THE MOVIE STORYBOOK

By JANE B. MASON

Based on the motion picture screenplay by DAVID KOEPP
and the novel *THE LOST WORLD* by MICHAEL CRICHTON

GROSSET & DUNLAP • NEW YORK

In the Pacific Ocean, not far from Costa Rica, lies a lush tropical island. The island is covered with thick jungle foliage and a deep, dense fog. It is called Isla Sorna.

People do not live on Isla Sorna, and local fishermen do not venture too close to its shores. Because if you cast your nets off Isla Sorna's misty coast, you may never be seen again....

In a city in the United States, far away from Isla Sorna, John Hammond was talking to an old friend. Mr. Hammond was the creator of Jurassic Park, an island where real, live dinosaurs walked the earth. But before the park could open, there had been a terrible accident. The dinosaurs were too dangerous. The park had been destroyed.

"Come in, Ian," Hammond said warmly. "Come in!"

Scientist Ian Malcolm stepped into Hammond's room. "You wanted to see me...?" Ian began.

"Yes," said Hammond, smiling. "I know we've had our differences, Ian. But I've changed my ways, and now I need your help...on Site B."

Ian looked concerned. He remembered the terrifying dinosaurs from Jurassic Park. A lot of people had died. And it had been John Hammond's fault. Was the man going to let it happen again?

Hammond began to explain. "Jurassic Park was just a showroom, you see. We bred the dinosaurs on another island—Site B—eighty miles away. But not long after the Jurassic Park...um, accident...a hurricane destroyed Site B. We had to evacuate everyone and leave the animals to mature on their own. Now they all live there together—naturally. No fences. No human interference. Exactly the way they lived millions of years ago!"

Ian shook his head. Clearly the man had not learned anything. "What do you want with me?" he asked.

"I want to protect the dinosaurs. So I'm sending in a team to document them," Hammond replied. "A photographer, an equipment specialist, a paleontologist...and hopefully you."

Ian eyed Hammond with dread. "Who is the paleontologist?" he asked.

"Sarah Harding," said John Hammond. "In fact, she's already there."

Ian's face turned white. Not only was Sarah Harding the best paleontologist in the field, she was Ian's girlfriend.

"Are you crazy?" he exclaimed. "This is not a research mission anymore, John. It's a rescue mission, and I'm leading it!"

That night, Ian met with the two other men on the mission. Eddie Carr was the equipment specialist, and Nick van Owen was the photographer. Ian insisted that they leave immediately. He even asked his twelve-year-old daughter, Kelly, to meet him at the warehouse so he could tell her good-bye.

Kelly looked at him suspiciously. "You're going away again," she guessed. Her shoulders slumped. First her parents divorced and her mom moved to Paris without her. Now her dad kept traveling on business. "Can I come with you?" she asked hopefully.

Ian shook his head. "I'm sorry."

Kelly watched her dad walk across the warehouse. It was full of all sorts of vehicles, catwalks, and electronic equipment. Off to one side were two trailers connected by an accordion-like middle. Curious, Kelly walked over to it.

Looking around to make sure no one was watching, Kelly slipped inside. The trailers were filled with computers and lab equipment, and a large map on one wall lit up from behind. It showed the country of Costa Rica—and some of the islands off its coast.

Kelly wondered if these trailers were going on the expedition with her dad.

The next day, a huge ocean barge loaded with equipment pulled up to Isla Sorna. It unloaded its cargo—the three men, their trailers, and two all-activity vehicles—and headed back out to sea.

Ian, Eddie, and Nick drove to a high, grassy plain and made camp. Then they set off on foot to look for Sarah.

Eddie turned on a small monitor and watched it begin to blink. "This tracking device will lead us right to her," he said. Then he noticed the trees around them begin to sway. "What in the...?"

Suddenly a row of fins appeared above the foliage. Then a second, smaller pair came into view.

Stegosaurs!

The earth vibrated, and a third Stegosaurus lumbered out of the bushes right behind them. It followed the other dinosaurs to a small clearing.

Ian, Eddie, and Nick stepped up to the clearing and blinked in surprise. They were looking at a whole herd of stegosaurs!

At the end of the clearing, Sarah knelt, taking pictures. When she saw the three men, she smiled and waved.

"She's gutsy," Nick said, impressed.

"She's nuts," Ian replied.

"This is—this is magnificent!" Eddie exclaimed in awe.

Ian shook his head. "Yeah, 'oooh,' 'aaah.' That's how it always starts. Screaming and running come later."

Smiling, Sarah turned and made her way toward a baby Stegosaurus—until she was close enough to touch it. She snapped picture after picture, finishing up the roll. Then she hurried over to the men.

"Ian! Did you see those animals that just walked by? It was a family group. The hatchlings definitely stay in the birth environment for an extended time!"

Ian gritted his teeth and took Sarah aside. "Okay, okay. You've seen the place. You've proven your theories. Now it's time to go."

But Sarah shook her head. "It's more than that," she said. "At last I have the chance to prove that dinosaurs really were nurturing parents."

"They were also killers," Ian said.

"If we stay off the game trails, we'll be fine," Sarah replied calmly. "I've worked with predators for years. I know what I'm doing."

Ian decided to wait until they returned to camp to argue with Sarah any further. But by then he was in for an even greater surprise. Kelly Malcolm was waiting in the trailer!

"I was just making dinner," she said happily.

But Ian was furious. "Kelly, you have no idea what's going on here," he scolded. Then he turned to Sarah. "I'm taking my daughter out of here," he told her. "This is your last chance to get out, too."

Just then, a low sound echoed off the ocean, as the ground beneath them began to shake. Three huge military helicopters soared over their heads. The name of John Hammond's company, InGen, was written on their sides.

"That's odd," said Sarah. "Why would Mr. Hammond send *two* teams here?"

"He didn't," Ian replied, as he watched the choppers land and the first man step out. "It's Peter Ludlow."

Peter Ludlow was John Hammond's nephew. He was also the new president of Hammond's company. But unlike Hammond, who wanted to protect the dinosaurs, Peter Ludlow wanted to use them to make money—regardless of the danger.

From their campsite on the high ridge above, Ian and the others watched Peter Ludlow's group hop into safari vehicles and take off into the jungle. They were going to capture dinosaurs—and take them back to the United States. Within minutes, they were chasing a mixed herd of herbivores.

The man leading the hunt, Roland Tembo, barked orders into his radio: "Break that pacha...pachy...that big bald one off the herd and flush him right!"

A motorcycle zoomed off to corner the frightened animal, as a hunter in another jeep raised his tranquilizer gun and fired. The Pachycephalosaurus staggered and someone tossed a lasso around its neck. They reeled the dinosaur in. Then two giant mechanical arms lifted it into the back of a truck.

Nearby, Roland and his tracker, Ajay, got out of their jeep to study a huge footprint on the ground. It was very deep, with three toe marks. Tyrannosaurus rex!

Roland's eyes narrowed behind his dark glasses. He'd come on this trip for one reason and one reason only: to hunt the fiercest predator that ever lived. Without a word, Roland walked over to his jeep and got his gun.

Ajay led the way, and soon the two men had followed the tracks to the mouth of a cave. Animal bones were scattered everywhere. Some were still covered with rotting flesh.

A strange, high-pitched squeaking came from inside the cave. Crawling forward, the two men peered over the top of a mud wall.

On the other side was a baby—a baby Tyrannosaurus rex! The wall was actually part of a ten-foot nest. The scruffy infant looked up at the men and squeaked angrily.

All at once, Roland got an idea.

Later that night, Roland explained to the others how he had chained the baby rex to a stake in the clearing near the hunters' base camp.

Peter Ludlow looked at him in surprise. "Do you really think that will draw the adult?" he asked. "A T-rex doesn't care about its young!"

Just then something scampered out of the bush behind him. Startled, Peter spun around...and accidentally stepped on the baby's leg.

CRACK! The fragile bone snapped right in half. The baby howled.

Roland shoved Peter aside. "You've broken its leg!" he growled.

Later, on a ridge above the hunters' camp, Ian, Kelly, Sarah, Nick, and Eddie watched as Ludlow prepared to broadcast a report back to his board of directors, complete with pictures of the live specimens they had collected—compys, stegos, Triceratops, all safely stowed in cages.

Somehow, they knew they could not let Ludlow take these dinosaurs back to the mainland—no matter what. So they devised a plan. Nick and Sarah would sneak into the camp and cut the gas lines on the jeeps, then move on to the dinosaur cages. One by one, they would open them all.

Moments later, the hunters were screaming as an enormous Triceratops charged through their tents. Dinosaurs raced through the campsite, trampling everything in their paths. Another Triceratops thundered into a jeep, sending it rolling into the campfire.

KERRPOW! The jeep exploded. Fire and smoke shot into the jungle air.

As they ran back to their own vehicle, Sarah and Nick came across the wounded baby rex. Knowing it could not survive on its own with a broken leg, they brought it back to their camp. Inside the trailer, the baby rex howled in pain.

Kelly was worried. "Other animals are going to hear this, aren't they?" she said. "I want to get out of here before they come after it!"

So Ian and Eddie took her to the high hide, a metal cage mounted on a tall scaffold. Fifteen feet above the ground, they were safe from the dinosaurs. But even from way up there, they could hear the baby rex. SCREEECH!

ROOAAARRR! Suddenly, something answered the baby from the jungle.

Ian climbed down from the high hide. He had to warn Sarah! He burst into the trailer just as she finished splinting the baby's leg. But before they could get the baby out of the trailer, a deafening roar sounded right outside the door.

Ian, Nick, and Sarah all froze as the mother rex peered into the trailer's barred window. The huge dinosaur began to gurgle and coo. And the baby gurgled back

ROAR! Just then, a deafening bellow came from the other side of the trailer. There were *two* tyrannosaurs out there!

"Here come Mommy and Daddy," Ian whispered.

"They've come for their baby!" Sarah said.

Very slowly, Ian opened the door and pushed the baby out toward its waiting parents. The rexes snuffled and cooed as they inspected their infant. And as Ian watched through the window, they headed back into the forest.

Ian, Sarah, and Nick sighed in relief. But minutes later—

WHAM! Something smashed into the side of the trailer. It flipped upside down, then lurched forward. The dinosaurs were back! They pushed the trailer toward a steep cliff, and soon it was dangling over the edge.

Sarah lost her grip and slid down toward the trailer's broken rear window. She blinked and looked down. There was nothing but ocean—five hundred feet below! Already terrified of heights, Sarah screamed and closed her eyes.

Outside, the dinosaurs lumbered back into the jungle once again. And suddenly everything was quiet.

Then a voice called from above them. "Hello?!" It was Eddie! He tossed a rope down to the trailer, then hooked it up to one of the AAV's. He had come to tow the trailer to safety.

Eddie hopped behind the driver's seat and hit the gas. The engine roared...and a roar from the jungle answered back. But Eddie didn't hear it.

He stepped on the gas again—just as the two tyrannosaurs burst out of the jungle. With a mighty bite, they snatched Eddie up and retreated back into the trees, and the trailer went sliding over the cliff.

Luckily, Sarah, Ian, and Nick still had the rope Eddie had tossed them. They clung to it as the trailer fell past them, leaving them dangling in midair.

Exhausted, they tried to climb up to the edge of the cliff. But the rain-soaked rope was too slippery. Then, out of nowhere, three hands appeared above them. Roland and two other hunters had heard the commotion and come to help.

Ian, Sarah, and Nick were safe.

The survivors fetched Kelly from the high hide and regrouped at the hunters' camp. By now the rain had stopped. But with all their equipment destroyed, neither crew could continue its original mission. Instead, they'd have to work together just to get off the island at all.

They now had no way to communicate with the outside world. Their only chance, Ludlow told them, would be to hike to the abandoned communications center in the middle of the island and try to call for help.

The group walked through the night and all the next day. As night fell, they reached a ridge. They were almost there.

"We'll eat first and sleep, then go on," Roland ordered.

Soon a camp was made and a couple of tents were pitched. Ian settled Sarah and Kelly down in one. But when Sarah hung up her damp shirt to dry, she noticed a wide streak of blood across the front. It was blood from the baby rex!

The next thing they knew—BMBBB! BMBBB!—the mother T-rex was outside the tent. She had picked up the scent.

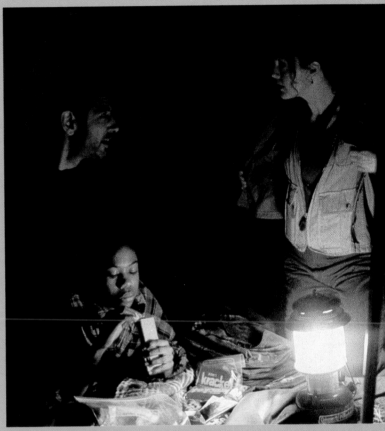

Sarah and Kelly dove into Sarah's sleeping bag. As they zipped it closed, the tyrannosaur's head poked in through the tent flap. She sniffed the sleeping bag and the shirt. Then she turned back toward the hunters, who were running for their lives—all but Roland.

Calmly, he slid a pair of tranquilizer darts into his gun, snapped it shut, and watched as the rex began to charge....

Meanwhile, a second T-rex—the father—had stepped out of the forest. He chased down the fleeing hunters, gulping down one and trampling another.

Desperate, one group of hunters plunged into a field of long grass.

"The rexes gave up," one of them said hopefully, looking around.

"They're not chasing us!" said another.

But the hunters didn't see the three dinosaur heads rise up from the grass behind them. Or the grass begin to ripple as, one by one, the hunters were dragged down.

Velociraptors! The hunters had entered their feeding grounds.

A little while later, Kelly, Sarah, Ian, and Nick ran into the same field. Tall grass closed around them just as Ian heard a familiar snarl. Whirling around, he saw the grass quiver.

"Go! Fast!" Ian shouted.

Running at top speed, the group made their way out of the grass. But a raptor was right behind them. And more were closing in.

Then all of a sudden, the ground dropped away beneath them. They fell down a steep hillside, tumbling out of control. Battered and scratched, they slowly rose to their feet and looked around. The raptors were gone.

"Look!" Sarah said, staring at something in the distance. It was the remains of the worker village.

Nick grabbed a big flashlight. "I'll run ahead and find the communication center," he told the others, "and try to send a radio call for help."

Nick raced into the worker village and down the deserted streets. The hurricane had destroyed most of the buildings, and the jungle had grown over everything that remained. Luckily, the operations building was still intact and the geothermal power generator still worked.

Soon Nick was in the communications room. Holding his breath, he flipped the switches. And one by one, the radio lights flickered on.

By the time Ian, Kelly, and Sarah reached the village, a loud roar was echoing around them. A helicopter!

But before they could get to it, another roar sounded, and a raptor leaped out at them.

Quickly, they dove into the closest building—a tall, broken-down shed.

"Can you climb this stuff?" Sarah asked Kelly, pointing to the catwalks above them.

Kelly didn't answer. She just started to climb. Sarah and Ian followed, but the next thing they knew, a raptor appeared behind Ian, ready to spring!

Kelly spotted a bar running from one wall to the other. Leaping into space, she grabbed hold of the bar and spun over the top. She let go, flying feet first at the raptor. Her feet hit the beast square in the side, and sent the raptor hurtling through space and into a metal wall.

Together, Ian and Kelly jumped down to the dirt floor, while Sarah kept climbing toward a high window.

"Take the roof to the chopper and we'll meet you there," Ian called to her.

Sarah obeyed. CRASH! She kicked out the window and climbed onto a slanted tile roof. But a raptor was right behind her, and another one was waiting below!

Frantic, Sarah tossed broken roof tiles at the raptors until an avalanche of tiles tumbled down. The raptor on the roof slid off—right onto the other one. In that second, Sarah dropped to the street below.

Together again, Ian, Kelly, and Sarah ran to the helicopter, where Nick was already waiting. At last, they were safe.

As the helicopter flew over the island, Sarah leaned over to the window for one last look...and her face went pale.

Below them, at the ruined campsite, lay a tranquilized Tyrannosaurus rex. Roland Tembo hovered over it, fitting a giant harness around its body. Beside it, Peter Ludlow stood with the injured baby rex in his arms. And near the island's shore, a powerful barge waited to transport them.

Somehow Ludlow had contacted help, too, and now he was taking the Tyrannosaur back to the United States.

"Okay, now I'm mad!" said Ian.

A few days later, Peter Ludlow stood at a huge waterfront complex in California, addressing a group of InGen executives—and, unknown to him, Ian and Sarah.

His words drifted off as a low rumble echoed in the harbor. The crowd screamed and took off in all directions as a boat thundered toward them at full speed! It crashed into the pier, ripping it in half. Then it hit an electrical transformer and the whole waterfront was plunged into darkness.

Two waterfront guards climbed aboard the ship. Ian, Sarah, and Peter were right behind them.

CLANG! The two cargo-hold doors shot open, and the mother tyrannosaur sprang onto the deck! With two more steps and a leap, she landed on the dock below and took off into the night.

Sarah knew that somehow they had to lure the tyrannosaur back to the boat. But what could they use as bait?

The infant!

"Where is the baby?" she shouted.

By the time Peter Ludlow had told Ian and Sarah where to find the baby rex, the adult was roaming freely through the city. She was just about to attack a group of people, when she stopped and sniffed the air.

SCREEECH! Ian, Sarah, and the baby rex skidded to a halt in front of the rex. Turning their car around, Ian hit the gas, hard. The dinosaur took off after them. She wanted her baby!

CHOMP! As the mother rex lifted the rear of the car off the ground, Sarah grabbed the baby rex and leaped out of the car. She raced to the dock and onto the ship, and the mother followed...all the way into the open hold.

Then, as the mother lovingly nuzzled her infant, Sarah picked up a tranquilizer gun, aimed, and fired....

The beast was contained.

A few days later, Ian, Kelly, and Sarah sat, safe in their living room, watching a huge ocean barge on the evening news. It was headed for Isla Sorna. Inside its cargo hold, the mother rex slept peacefully, her baby by her side. The dinosaurs were being returned to their home to live in peace.

Still, people would always remember what had happened on the island and in California. And no one would ever forget the terrifying power of the beasts who had returned to Earth from a Lost World.